I0621873

A SINFUL STRIPTEASE

(The Sin Club Book 1)

RACHELLE CHASE

Copyright © 2007, 2015 by Rachelle Chase

First published in the USA by Kensington Publishing, 2007

Cover Design: Kevin Plottner and Rachelle Chase
Cover Photography: Fotolia and iStock

All rights reserved. This book or any portion thereof may not be reproduced or used in any manner whatsoever without the express written permission of the author except for the use of brief quotations in a book review.

This book is a work of fiction. All characters and events that appear in this work are fictitious and the result of the author's imagination. Any resemblance to real persons, living or dead, is purely coincidental.

Printed in the United States of America

ISBN-10: 0-9864-2421-8
ISBN-13: 978-0-9864242-1-2

ACKNOWLEDGMENTS

Special thanks to my family for their belief, trust, and love . . . Leigh Michaels, for being my friend and colleague, as well as patiently listening to my zillionth "brilliant" idea . . . Saeeda Hafiz for continuing to answer the phone when I call . . . and to readers, for continuing to read my books.

PROLOGUE

Transcript of interview with Dr. Tommy "Love" Jones on San Francisco's #1 morning television show, *Wake Up Bay Area:*

Wake Up Bay Area *theme song plays in the background. A red leather couch flanked by two brown suede chairs is situated in front of a floor-to-ceiling backdrop of the Golden Gate Bridge. Dr. Tommy "Love" Jones, wearing a black scoop-neck T-shirt and khaki pants, sits on the couch, arms spread along the back, legs crossed, looking out at the audience with a smile.*

Glass-topped coffee table, empty except for a red ceramic coffee cup, sits immediately in front of Dr. Love.

Wake Up Bay Area *cohost Lisa Mann, dressed in a powder-blue suit, sits in the chair to the right, diagonal to the couch, with her legs crossed, coffee cup in hand, smiling faintly, her profile to the camera.*

Music ends.

ANNOUNCER: Wake up, Bay Area!

LISA: *(to audience)* Good morning, Bay
                 Area. Today, we'll be talking with
                 Dr. Tommy "Love" Jones, host
                 of the popular radio talk show,
                 The Sin Club.

                 (turns to Dr. Love) Welcome, Dr.
                 Love.

DR. LOVE: *(smiles)* Thank you, Lisa.

LISA: *The Sin Club*—such an interesting
                 name. I know our viewers are
                 dying to know the answer to this
                 question: How did *The Sin Club*
                 get its start?

DR. LOVE: *(laughs)* By accident. When I took
                 over the midnight show at KPSX
                 several months ago, I kept the
                 format open. Listeners could call in
                 and talk about whatever was on
                 their mind. Before long, I noticed a
                 pattern. More than half of the folks
                 seemed to be calling in with
                 relationship problems. So I focused
                 the show on relationship
                 empowerment and called the show

2

The Sin Club.

LISA: *(frowns)* But . . . The Sin Club . . . what does that have to do with relationships or empowerment?

DR. LOVE: *(leans forward, his expression serious)* Most people who called in were unhappy in their relationships, but rather than doing anything about it, they settled—and complained. So I encouraged them to "sin."

What's the accepted definition of "to sin"?—to commit an offense. To these people who were settling and complaining, taking action to solve the relationship problem was offensive to them.

So my definition of "to sin" is to take action. To go after what you want. If you're not happy in your relationship, do something about it. If your partner is not treating you right, don't accept it. If your old methods of getting what you want are not working, try new ones. If you want that man or that woman, go after him or her. *(laughs)* Well, only if you're both single.

LISA: *(nods and sips coffee)* You make it sound so simple.

DR. LOVE: It is. Deep down inside, I believe people know what they want, know what they should do. They know when they should leave a relationship and they know when they should stay. Part of "sinning" is listening to that little voice, breaking out of your comfort zone, and taking action.

LISA: If it's so simple, why is your show so popular? *(leans forward, sets cup on the table, and grabs her notepad, reading notes)*. I mean, in less than three months your show has gone nationwide. Your midnight broadcast is replayed twice daily. *(looks up)* Why can't people heed your advice on their own?

DR. LOVE: *(shrugs)* Why do people with a drinking problem join Alcoholics Anonymous? Or people with a weight problem join Weight Watchers? For support. Whenever you're trying to break a habit, it helps to have encouragement. *The Sin Club* is a safe, anonymous environment for people to get the encouragement they need to make hard decisions—and to report back on their success and failures.

With 50 percent of all marriages ending in divorce and about half of those who remain married being in unhappy marriages—not to mention the single folks in bad relationships—unhappy relationships are a big part of American society. That's why *The Sin Club* is so popular.

LISA: Unfortunately, we're out of time. Is there any advice you'd like to leave our viewers with?

DR. LOVE: *(grins)*. Yes. Go sin.

LISA: *(chuckles)*. All right. Great advice. Thank you for taking the time to chat with us today, Dr. Love.

DR. LOVE: Thank you, Lisa. It was a pleasure to be here.

LISA: *Wake Up Bay Area* will be back after these messages from our sponsors.

Wake Up Bay Area theme song plays in the background. Dr. Love is leaning forward, forearms resting on his knees, listening to Lisa. Lisa is talking, gesturing with her hand. Dr. Love nods and laughs, then begins talking.

Music ends.

Cut to commercial.

1

"*Today* is the day to sin . . ." Dr. Tommy "Love" Jones's voice seemed to whisper the words directly into Jessie Anderson's ear.

Jessie turned from the window and frowned at the stereo speaker from which Dr. Love spoke. "I'm *trying* to sin," she muttered.

"Take charge—" continued Dr. Love.

"I am."

"Be bold—"

"I am."

"Do something you've never done before—"

"I am!"

"—something that you've always wanted to do, but never thought you could do. Because you were too scared to go after it. Or scared you might actually get it—"

"I'm not scared I'll get it."

"—Or scared you might *not* get it."

"Yeah, well, I am a bit scared of that one."

"So be bold. Take charge. Do it. Go sin. It's all

about you . . .Tonya M., you're on the air."

Jessie turned her attention back to the window. She parted the gauzy curtain, careful to keep her nakedness hidden. As she peeked outside, she idly listened to the radio show. As Tonya M. described her deep-seated desire to give up psychiatry and become a mortician—and how her career unhappiness was affecting her relationship—Jessie shook her head. Why did the grass always look greener? Here Tonya wanted to flee the living and work with the dead, while all Jessie wanted to do was inject some life, some excitement, some *sex* into a member of the walking dead: Martin.

And today—tonight—was her last chance to save their relationship.

Jessie reached over and switched the radio off. She turned on her iPod. Sade's "Ordinary Love" soothed her frazzled nerves as she gazed out the window, ignoring the beauty of the ocean below. Instead, her gaze sought the backyard of the vacant single-story house next door. She stared intently into the blackness, able to make out the dark shadow that was the gazebo, nothing more.

No flicker of red light.

Jessie dropped the curtain and began to pace, her quick strides causing the flames of twenty candles to flutter erratically as she passed.

Where was Martin? He should have arrived more than thirty minutes ago. She was sure her written instructions had been clear: *Be at the gazebo of the vacant house next door. Flash the light on your key chain at 9:00 P.M. sharp.* Though Martin was a genius with numbers, erotic rendezvous were not his forte. But surely even Martin couldn't screw that up?

Maybe his penlight had gone out.

Heart racing with anticipation, body thrumming with excitement, Jessie rushed back to the window. Was that the signal? She craned her neck. Yes, a definite red flicker. She took a deep breath.

Take charge.

Be bold.

Do it.

Go sin.

Summoning the sexy vixen sleeping within, Jessie smiled in the direction of the signal, and flung open the curtains.

~~~~

Nick Ralston gazed out over the ocean, admiring the moonlight as it bounced off the waves. He loved the sound of the ocean, so peaceful, so different from his life. But that was about to change. Making a fresh start wasn't going to be easy, but he'd taken the first step by buying this house. His house. Well, technically it wasn't his yet, but it would be by next Friday. For added insurance, maybe the "For Sale" sign out front would mysteriously disappear when he left. He smiled at the image of the large sign hanging out of the passenger side of his Porsche Boxster.

Leaning against the gazebo, Nick lit a Marlboro Light. He exhaled the smoke before it could enter his lungs and withdrew the cigarette from his lips, staring at the glowing tip. With a wry smile, he flicked his wrist and sent the cigarette spiraling to the damp grass. He ground the toe of his shoe against it, extinguishing it forever. He sighed. No women, and now, no cigarettes. Which one would prove harder to swear off?

With one last glance at the ocean, he turned to

walk down the path separating his house from his neighbor's, heading to his car. He'd only taken two steps when a movement in the second story window of the neighboring house caught his eye. He glanced up and stopped in mid-stride.

A woman in a red see-through number stood in the window, silhouetted against a backdrop of flickering candles. Nick watched her lean forward and open the window. Muted strains of drums, guitar, and piano drifted over to him, accompanied by a sultry feminine voice. It took him a moment to realize that the throaty lyrics were not recorded with the music, but rather, were coming from the woman herself.

As she straightened, the hot curves of her body were once again visible. The bouncing light shone through the thin material, perfectly outlining the small waist and flaring hips that merged into lush thighs. Thighs that parted and hips that began to gyrate suggestively as he watched.

"What the hell . . .?"

As if in answer to his question, the woman took a step backward into the room. Candlelight illuminated her face enough for Nick to see her lips curl into a seductive smile. He watched her long, slender arms rise above her head, her wrists and shoulders rotating in sync with her hips. Her fingertips slowly traveled down her body, brushing lightly over her breasts, over her stomach, down her thighs, then back up, this time caressing her inner thighs and taking the hem of her gown with them. His breath stuttered in his throat as her hands stopped at her pussy, her fingertips making vertical circles while her hips moved back and forth to meet them.

Nick's hand went to his crotch.

The urge to unzip his jeans and stroke himself in time to the woman's swaying hips surged through him. Instead, he moved his cock to a more comfortable position. He knew he should leave. But, he couldn't. Her hips mesmerized him, keeping him rooted to the spot. Unlike the erotic acts he'd been forced to endure at bachelor parties, this woman's routine seemed . . . personal. Her movements unpracticed, spontaneous and aimed directly at him, at his satisfaction. He didn't know why or how she even knew he was here.

But, hell, did he really care?

Her fingers stopped their lazy circling, the clingy material dropping back into place around her thighs.

"No . . ." Nick's whisper of dismay escaped him of its own volition.

Ignoring his need, the woman buried her hands in her upswept hair. A quick shake and ebony curls cascaded over her shoulders. She threw her head back, drawing Nick's eyes to her throat, infusing him with the desire to trail his lips along her neck, down to her shoulders, to nibble at her collarbone before licking—

His visual fantasy ended abruptly as her head snapped forward and she crooned to the waning music. Her lips—coated a shiny red that shimmered with each word she sang—plucked a chord tied directly to his cock. A smile spread slowly over her face, as if she knew exactly what was happening to Nick. Then she spun around and sashayed to a chair he hadn't even noticed was in the room. Her back to him, she shimmied in front of the chair, her hands grabbing her ass, squeezing and massaging, her fiery nails glistening with each grasp.

Nick licked his lips and reached in his back pocket for the emergency cigarette before remembering it lay mutilated in the grass.

He let his hand fall back to his side.

The music changed to something slower and the piano was replaced by electronic keyboards. As the moody notes of a saxophone cascaded over his eardrums, the woman's hands caressed their way up her back and slid the straps of her gown over her shoulders.

Nick held his breath, waiting, hoping, praying . . .

As if in slow motion, he watched the slinky material slide over her skin, hugging her hips for the briefest moment, before gliding to the floor.

His erection surged against his jeans as he stared at the most perfect ass he'd ever seen. No anorexic model here. This one would give Marilyn Monroe or J.Lo a run for her money. Before he could look his fill at her backside, she turned around and Nick's mouth dropped open.

She was holding a stuffed bear. Only this was no innocent bear from Saturday morning cartoons.

She trailed the bear's face over her body, giving the impression it was bestowing kisses, licking and laving its way across her breasts. She held its head against one breast and rubbed it slightly back and forth.

Nick groaned. An unbidden desire surfaced to feel her hands threaded through his hair, pressing his face against her plump tits, to let his tongue flick across her dusky nipples, to feel them harden in his mouth . . .

He watched her change the bear's position, dragging it across her abdomen, lower, lower . . .

His breath became ragged. "Oh yeah . . . that's it,"

he breathed, as she brought the bear's face to the place that Nick desperately wanted to see, to explore.

Suddenly, she turned around, her back once again to him. The bear's lower body dangled obscenely between the "v" of her thighs as she threw her head back and rotated her hips.

Nick closed his eyes, blocking out the sight of her full derriere swaying back and forth. He inhaled deeply and concentrated on getting his pulse and hormones back under control. He had to get out of there.

Now.

He'd ignore her. He'd walk back to his car, not once looking up at that window. Yeah, that's what he'd do.

He opened his eyes and took his first step with determination. By the second step, he felt his eyes drawn back to the window. Okay, he'd take one last look while he was walking. Before he'd completed his third step, he stopped and gaped at the window.

The bear had disappeared and the woman stood gloriously naked. Her finger curled and uncurled, beckoning. She turned, smiling at him over her shoulder, then moved from sight.

Nick remained where he was, stunned. This woman—this stranger—had just invited him inside.

His first thought was to take her up on her offer, to run, not walk, right up to that second-story bedroom. But the voice of reason intervened, reminding him of his promise:

No women.

Sandy, hooking him with her flirtatious ways, keeping him with her passion and adoration, and sinking him with her lies, had been the perfect catalyst for his vow. While he'd been walking around proud to be her man, she'd been making other men proud— teasing them, leading them on, and sleeping with them.

No. He had no time for women, no time to try and figure out who was telling the truth and who was lying. He was here to focus on work.

No women.

Silently repeating the promise like a mantra, Nick continued along the path and stalked to the front of the house, determined to ignore the images of his naked neighbor and what she might be doing in bed—without him. When he reached the driveway, he opened the car door and paused. He turned around and glanced back at the now-empty window.

His cock still throbbed. His pulse still raced. Curiosity and anger battled in his mind.

Why the fuck had this sexy stranger beckoned *him?*

2

Jessie picked up the silk scarf from the bed, looped it around her head, and tied it in the back. She adjusted the silky material so that the world was black, the dancing flames gone as if she'd blown them out. She lay on her back on the bed, resting her head against the pillow, and raised one leg, bending it at the knee.

Her body tingled. Every nerve ending under her skin had been awakened by her hands as they'd traced her hips, trailed over her abdomen, and cupped her breasts. Desire, anticipation, and a hint of embarrassment coursed through her veins—a tinge of embarrassment because she'd never been so bold, never acted so brazen, never felt so sexy.

She'd implemented Dr. Love's advice. She was sinning.

But Martin had never seen this side of her before—would he like it?

Jessie frowned. What man wouldn't like it? Countless men's magazines—and women's, for that matter—were devoted to ways of spicing up your sex life. And hers and Martin's had disappeared. If this didn't infuse a bit of excitement, it would be the sign she'd been looking for, final proof that there was no relationship left to salvage.

Your relationship was over months ago. Sex isn't going to save it.

Jessie shifted her hips, crushing the thought, and letting the softness of the comforter caress her ass.

The soft whisper of the front door opening caressed her eardrums.

Footsteps, muted by the runners covering the hardwood stairs, sent anticipation humming through her body. Maybe she'd been wrong about Martin. Maybe there was something left in their relationship.

Jessie cocked her head. She couldn't see through the blindfold, but the creak of the floor told her that Martin stood in the doorway.

"Hi," she purred.

Martin remained silent.

Her body flamed, excited by the thought of Martin speechless. She arched her back and rotated her hips slowly. "Do you like what you see?"

He inhaled sharply.

She slid her hands over her breasts, plucking a nipple. Darts of delicious prickles zoomed to her pussy. She moved her hands lower and cupped her mound.

Martin exhaled noisily.

Jessie lifted her hips. "Pussy got your tongue?"

She chuckled at her pun.

He didn't laugh. The only sound was the sigh of his uneven breathing.

He didn't move. Tension emanated from his body

and spiraled through the air and stroked her body, empowering her, arousing her.

Jessie returned one hand to her chest, circling her breast. "Did you like watching Teddy lick my nipples?" With her other hand, she rubbed a finger along her clit. "Did you like watching Teddy taste my pussy?"

Her hips rose, beckoning him closer.

The floor in the doorway creaked again as he obeyed. The whisper of fabric brushing together started—then abruptly stopped—at the side of the bed.

Jessie looked up at him with eyes unable to see, imagining his eyes roving her body, seeing flushed skin, her turgid nipples, and her wet pussy.

The bed dipped to the right with his weight.

"I want you to—"

Martin's fingertips silenced her as he traced her mouth and down her neck, to the swell of her breasts, following the path hers had made. The pads of his thumbs rubbed her nipples.

"Oh," she breathed, jutting her breasts forward into his palms. "I like that. It's been a long time since you've touched me, Martin."

The fingertips left her skin abruptly.

"Don't stop."

He remained unmoving.

"Martin?"

He remained silent.

Oh shit. Don't tell me he's chickening out. If he was, this was it—officially the last straw. Jessie frowned and sat up, her hands going to her blindfold. "What—"

"Shhhhh—" Martin whispered. His hands pressed against her shoulders, gently pushing.

Jessie sank back onto the soft downy bed.

Martin leaned forward. She inhaled the faint scent of cigarette smoke and spicy cologne she'd never known him to wear before. Maybe he'd bought it for this occasion.

She smiled. "You smell good. Did you—"

His mouth replaced his fingertips, interrupting her thoughts as he nibbled her neck. His tongue traced her collarbone and moved down, dipping in between the valley of her breasts, before turning inward and circling her areola.

Jessie moaned. "Oh, I like that."

She moved her hands to his shoulders.

His hands instantly circled her wrists, pulling them away, returning them to the side of the bed by her head.

She got the message—he wanted her to lie there and let him do whatever he wanted to do. The roughness of his hands gripping her wrists—so unlike their usual softness—sent a bolt of excitement swirling through her stomach. Her heart thrilled at the effort Martin was exerting to make this special. He was taking charge and playing along with her game.

It was more than she'd hoped for. Never would she have thought that he had it in him. Sex with him had always been so routine and predictable. But maybe she'd been too quick to judge. Maybe there was hope for their relationship. Maybe she hadn't done a good job of showing him what she wanted. Well, that was going to change. Starting—

Once again, Martin took her nipple in his mouth and sucked.

Jessie sucked in a mouthful of air.

Spears of heat spread through her breasts, building

in her stomach, and spilling over into her pussy.

Jessie wriggled her hips and arched her back higher, wanting to feel more of him against her than his lips. She wanted to grab his head and press him closer. She wanted to wrap her legs around his chest and pull him against her. What she didn't want was for him to stop, so she didn't touch him.

Instead, her hands grabbed fistfuls of the comforter and her hips rocked against the bed. "I want more," she begged.

His lips moved to her other breast.

Her hips bucked. "I want you to li . . ." *lick me.*

She caught herself before she said the words. Martin wasn't into oral sex—giving or receiving. They'd had numerous arguments about that. Despite his new willingness to play along, she wasn't going to open that can of worms. Things were going too well. Her body was buzzing with sensation, her skin straining to touch his, her pussy reaching for his cock, her limbs aching to circle him.

"I want you to fuck me," she said instead.

A groan rumbled in Martin's chest.

A shiver rippled through her, excitement humming through her body by his response to her first use of the F word with him.

His mouth left her breast, trailing over her stomach, alternately blowing hot and cold air, causing her skin to quiver.

Fabric rustled and the bed dipped more to the side, as the cloth of his shirt—cotton?—brushed her thighs seconds before he positioned himself between her legs. His knees inched her legs open wider while his lips nibbled lower, kissing her naked flesh.

"Martin . . ." she whispered in amazement. Oh, my

God. He was going to do it. "Oh, Martin . . ."

His hands slid under her ass, gripping each cheek.

His tongue darted between her lips, lapping her swollen clit.

His hair brushed against her inner thighs, caressing her with feather-like strokes as his tongue slid lower, entering her like a miniature cock.

The heat that had pooled in her stomach flooded her pussy, seeking the fire ignited by his lips, the flames stoked by his tongue.

Jessie thrust her hips forward, urging him deeper.

Martin answered her plea. His tongue rammed her pussy, his moustache slightly abrading her lips.

His hands massaged her ass, the calluses dotting his palm contributing to the roughness of his grip.

His head bobbed between her thighs, the silky strands of his hair caressing her flesh.

All of this caused the pressure inside Jessie to build and—

Jessie froze.

The orgasm—seconds away from exploding within her— evaporated.

Moustache.

Calluses.

Silky hair.

Seconds ago, the feel of these things caressing her skin had teased and aroused her. Now they repulsed her.

Martin did not have a mustache.

Martin's hands were smooth from working computer keys all day.

Martin's crew cut felt spiky—not silky—against her flesh.

Heart crashing against her ribs, Jessie jerked

upright and scooted towards the head of the bed. She yanked off the blindfold.

Through the "v" of her legs, chocolate brown eyes framed by long, dark lashes, stared back at her.

Nutmeg brown hair fell across his forehead.

His full, kissable lips glistened in the candlelight— glistened with her juices.

Jessie screamed.

3

Nick's sluggish brain grappled with the fact that his tongue no longer delved into hot flesh—no longer tasted the spicy muskiness of hot pussy—and quivering thighs no longer clutched his head.

He blinked, trying to focus on the terror-filled brown eyes staring back at him.

The high-pitched scream that nearly split his head in half cleared the fogginess from his brain, providing instant clarity.

He stood and backed away from the bed, holding his hands up halfway in a gesture of surrender.

Still screaming, the woman dove for the side of the bed, rummaged around under it, and stood. She gripped a Louisville Slugger baseball bat, her stance resembling a batter at home plate awaiting the pitcher's throw.

The sight of the naked, five-foot-three-inch tall woman clutching a bat almost bigger than she was, itching to knock him out of the room, should have made him smile. Granted, it would be a wary smile, because adrenaline might give her the strength to break a few of his bones, even if she couldn't send his ass flying from the room.

Instead, as Nick took in the tangled black curls spilling over her shoulders, his hands itched to bury themselves in her hair, pull her head back, and kiss the succulent lips he'd wanted to plunder when he'd had her blindfolded beneath him. Her heaving chest made him crave holding a breast in each hand, squeezing and massaging, while watching her nipples grow hard—

Hard.

Just like his cock.

He gave an inward snort of disgust. Rather than smiling or indulging in lust, what the sight of the small, naked woman trembling in front of him should instill was the desire to reassure her, to calm her.

"I'll use this," she warned, shaking the bat.

"I know," he lied, trying to prevent his eyes from noticing that the end of the bat was close to her flat stomach, inches from the baby smooth flesh that he'd been tasting. A hint of the clit he'd been probing peeked through her still-swollen lips.

His cock lengthened painfully.

Nick, once again, shifted his stance in an attempt to get comfortable.

The woman also shifted her stance, placing one leg in front of the other, pressing them tightly together as if attempting to hide from his gaze.

Just like Pinocchio's nose, his cock grew. Though it felt like feet, not inches.

Shit. Focus, Ralston.

He raised his gaze, noticing her arms clutched together, as if she were trying to hold the bat and hide her breasts at the same time.

Focus.

Nick lifted his hands higher in the air. "Look. I'm going to turn my back and risk you splattering my brains on this wall . . ." He turned and faced the doorway, praying his hunch that she wouldn't use his head as a baseball was right. "Now, cover yourself . . ."

All he heard was her jagged breathing.

". . . and let me know when it's safe . . ."

Safe for who? You or her?

". . . to turn around."

After seconds of continued silence, the rustle of clothing greeted his ears.

"Turn around," she said.

He turned.

She'd donned a red robe. The silky material clung to her hips, tracing her thighs and her mons, as if molded to her body by a slight current of static electricity. Her breasts tented the front of the robe, the nipples forming spiky peaks.

Obviously, her robe had done nothing to make either of them feel safer: Her ruby-tipped fingernails still gripped the bat; his rock hard cock still strained against his jeans.

Nick suppressed a sigh.

The only good sign was that anger had extinguished the terror that'd filled her eyes previously. This was a good sign because it meant progress had been made. The line between anger and passion was much easier to cross than that between terror and passion.

And Nick wanted to see her brown eyes sparkle with passion.

No women, remember?

Yeah, he'd remembered all the way across the yard to her front door, and up the stairs. He'd planned to march into the room and ask her what the hell she was doing. But when he'd stood in the doorway and stared at the luscious curves spread on the bed like a sinful buffet, he'd forgotten both his pledge and the plan.

"Who are you?"

"Nick Ralston." He smiled, hoping to put her at ease, then stuck out his arm, and took a step forward.

"Don't move." She waved the bat threateningly.

"Why don't you put the bat down?" He forced his voice lower, softer. "If I was here to hurt you, I could've done it a long time ago."

Her grip on the bat tightened. "What *are* you doing here?"

Good question, Ralston. "You invited me."

"I invited *Martin.*"

"Yeah, well, I didn't know that, did I?" *Well, not until later.* "Surely you don't think any man who saw your hot body gyrating naked in front of a window would be able to resist? . . ." Nick frowned. ". . . And just where is Martin?"

Color flooded her face. But based on her pursed lips, he guessed it was anger—not embarrassment—that had turned her cheeks rosy.

Her cheeks had been rosy minutes ago, too, when he'd been sampling her juices, but the pink hue sure as hell hadn't been due to anger or embarrassment.

Martin was obviously a fool. What man in his right mind would stand up such a hot, sexy, woman waiting for him?

A moronic asshole, that's who.

"Who's Martin?" the question slipped out, his tone sharper than he'd meant for it to be. And before he could stop them, a couple more words trickled out. "Your husband?"

Shit.

Prior to this moment, he hadn't considered the fact that she might be married. He made it a rule to never mess around with another man's—

"No, I'm—" Her mouth snapped shut and her chin jutted forward.

Nick smiled, relieved.

"But that's none of your business. The point is *you're* not Martin."

"No. I'm not Martin." Nick remembered her words when his fingertips had caressed her. "Unlike Martin, I touched you."

She gasped, drawing his eyes to her lips—lips that had been parted, just like they were now, when he'd been licking and kissing her other lips. Those lips had been parted, too. Partly by his tongue, as it'd slid from her pussy to her clit, but also because they'd been swollen.

Swollen with desire.

His cock swelled and he took a step forward.

"Don't." Her voice was shaky. Her grip loosened and the bat wavered.

He ignored her words, paying attention to the slight glaze in her eyes and the rapid rise of her chest, and took another step towards her. "Why's it been a long time since Martin's touched you?"

His slightest touch had sparked her body; she'd been on the verge of coming the second his lips— barely probing, hardly lathing—had caressed her hot flesh.

That knowledge had left him seconds from creaming his jeans—something he hadn't come close to doing since Honors English in junior high, when he'd fantasized about Ms. Jenkins giving him a blow job.

There was another possibility. "Is Martin impotent?"

"No!"

Nick took a final step until he was standing a couple feet in front of her, within batting distance. He wanted to lean down and kiss her, but the panic-mixed-with-lust expression on her face told him her response wouldn't be what he wanted. In fact, he might actually get clubbed by the bat, like she'd been promising. So instead, he reached out a hand and brushed his fingertips across her forehead and down her cheeks.

She inhaled sharply, drawing his eyes and his fingers to her mouth. He traced her upper lip. "When you asked, 'Do you like what you see?' my answer was . . ." He traced her lower lip. ". . . and still is, 'yes.'"

He trailed his finger over her chin and down her neck, feeling her throat bob as she swallowed. "And when you asked, 'Did you like watching Teddy lick my nipples . . .'"

He slid his fingers over the round swell of her breast and across her nipples.

She gasped.

"'. . . and taste my pussy?' my answer is yes."

He let his fingers follow the front of her robe, barely touching, past the sash, pausing at the bottom of her stomach. "I liked tasting your pussy. It was hot and spicy and sweet all rolled into one. And I want to taste it again."

He licked his lip, savoring the faint taste of her that lingered.

Her gaze dropped to his mouth, following the movement of his tongue. "Please. Leave."

Her whisper was strangled.

Yeah, Ralston. Leave. No women, remember?

Well, his plan was going to have to change. He'd stick to his pledge to give up cigarettes. How could any man—except Martin—be expected to hold out when presented with the luscious temptation in front of him? It'd be okay if he didn't give up *this* woman because this wasn't about a relationship.

She wouldn't get in the way of work.

If you say so, buddy.

His tone was determined. "When you realize Martin can't give you what you need, let me know."

He dropped his hand and stepped back. His cock was sending urgent messages to his brain—the command to take her in his arms, lead her back to the bed, and convince her to let him prove Martin's incompetence. He felt that she'd let him. The desire was rolling off her in waves, she was trembling with it, and he could smell her desire.

But the small twinge of guilt over the knowledge that he was encroaching on another man's territory—and taking advantage of her—pricked his conscience and forced him to keep walking. This had to be her decision, should she choose to get rid of Martin.

When she'd called you "Martin," why didn't you stop?

The sight of her blindfolded, gyrating her hips on the bed and touching her breasts, coupled with her words about that damn stuffed bear, had banished every thought from his head—except the desire to fuck her. And when he'd stroked her silky skin—

softly with feather-light caresses—and she'd begged him not to stop, he'd wanted to hear her beg him again. And again. And again.

When she'd called him Martin, he'd paused, and tried to gather the strength to stop, but . . .

Well, at least he hadn't had sex with her.

You fucking licked her cunt. What's that considered?

Well, he was walking away now, making up for it.

You fucking licked her cunt. Little late to be walking away now, isn't it? Might as well turn around and finish things.

He really had been planning to stop.

But he hadn't—and wouldn't have, had she not stopped him.

Turn around, man—she's yours now. What if she never dumps Martin?

4

Jessie ran down the hall and stopped at the top of the stairs, all the while keeping her eyes on the broad-shouldered stranger. He walked down the steps as if he didn't have a care in the world, as if he knew he was safe from the bat she still held. In fact, it wouldn't surprise her if he started whistling.

She should knock him upside the head just to prove that she could do it.

But she couldn't do it, nor did she *want* to do it. Instead, she wanted to call out to him and ask him to stop, to come back. God, what was wrong with her? A stranger had walked into her house, dipped his head between her legs, and used his tongue in places and ways that Martin never had.

Was she feeling outraged?

No.

Scared?

No.

How about violated?

No.

Instead, she felt confused and aroused. Nervous and aroused. Ashamed and aroused.

Aroused, aroused, and aroused.

Something seemed wrong with that. Like there should be a case study with her name on it in *Psychology Today.*

She watched him reach for the doorknob and turn it.

When you realize Martin can't give you what you need, let me know.

Martin hadn't given her what she needed—physically or emotionally—in months. She knew that but thought she'd make one last-ditch effort to rekindle . . . something.

Yeah, well, she'd rekindled something, all right. Just not with Martin.

Nick opened the door.

She gripped the banister with her free hand.

When you realize Martin can't give you what you need, let me know.

She didn't even know how to contact him, so how was she supposed to let him know what she needed? She shook her head in disgust. It was *good* that she didn't know his number or address because there was no way she was going to contact a man who, for all she knew, could be a pervert.

Then why was disappointment seeping into her cells and flooding her body?

The click of the door closing spurred her to race down the stairs. Jessie locked the door, engaging the lock in the doorknob, as well as the deadbolt. Then she peeked through the window to make sure he was, indeed, leaving.

The meager moonlight illuminated the faint

shadow of him on her stairs before the darkness swallowed him. She continued to stare into the blackness, straining for a sight of him, seconds before she heard the roar of a car engine in the driveway of the vacant house next door. Headlights snapped on, giving her a quick glimpse of a dark, sporty-looking car before he roared off into the night.

Jessie fell back against the door. Her body still hummed, but it wasn't with fear. Adrenaline pooled in her muscles, ready for action that had nothing to do with running.

Aroused, aroused, and aroused.

She closed her eyes. What was wrong with her?

5

Jessie opened her eyes, awakened by the flush of the toilet. She blinked several times and glanced around the room. When her eyes landed on the sputtering candles, she jerked upright.

Oh, God, had Nick come back? How could he have gotten back in her house? She'd watched him leave, saw him drive off, and had bolted the door.

The fear that she hadn't felt when she'd watched him leave flooded her system. Just as she scrambled out of bed, Martin came out of the bathroom in his white boxer shorts.

"Hi. Sorry I woke you," he said, yawning.

Jessie's heart stopped scrambling to break free of her chest. Taking in a deep, calming breath, she glanced at the clock. She'd been asleep for two hours—which meant it'd been two hours since she'd given a performance that should've had Martin rushing to her bed.

Only Martin hadn't seen it.

Surely you don't think any man who saw your hot body

gyrating naked in front of a window would be able to resist?

Images of the brown-haired stranger with sexy eyes and a lethal tongue, flickered through her mind. Of his mouth on her breasts, teasing her nipples, of his fingertips raking her thighs, making them quiver, of his tongue licking her flesh, bringing her to the cusp of orgasm.

Would Martin have done any of that, even if he had been there?

Her blood, once again, rushed through her veins. Anger and arousal swirled through her body. She pulled the silky robe closed and tightened the sash.

"What took you so long?" she asked, her tone deceptively calm.

"I had to work late." Martin's gaze flickered over her body, then he gestured towards the candles and frowned. "What are—"

"You had to work late."

Martin finally looked at her. His brows drew tighter together. "Yeah, you know about the audit next month. Smitherton wanted . . ."

Her blood crescendoed, drowning out the drone of his words. He'd foregone her stellar attempt to add some excitement to their nonexistent sex life for an audit? Not even bothering to call?

"Did you get my letter?" she asked.

"You mean the one the courier delivered?"

"I don't recall sending you another one. Did you read it?"

"I was going to but then Smitherton came in and . . ." he shrugged. ". . . well, you know how that is."

Yes, she did. Smitherton, Townsend, and Branson had been the cause of numerous late nights and cancelled weekend getaways.

Or so he'd said.

"I was going to open it, but I didn't think it was important."

"Martin, how often do I send letters to you at the office?"

He paused, studying her face. "Is this a trick question?"

"What?"

He sighed. "Okay. Never."

"Well, then, didn't it occur to you that it might be important?"

He glanced at the ceiling, as if seriously thinking about the question. Seconds later, his gaze returned to hers. "No."

Clueless, but honest. Gotta love that in a man. Or not.

Jessie tried a different approach. "Martin, can you remember when we last had sex?"

Martin's sigh was annoyed. "Oh, God, Jessie, not this again."

Jessie remained silent, waiting for his answer.

Martin raked his hand over his crew cut. "I think it was two months ago. That night you got me drunk."

"Exactly."

"Jessie, you know how hard Smitherton works me. I'm tired all the time and . . ." his tone was exasperated. ". . . who needs sex when we have . . . friendship."

"*I* need sex, Martin. And I'm not sure we have a friendship."

"What's that supposed to mean?"

"We don't talk—not about our day, not about our dreams, not about anything."

"That's not true. Why, just last week, we talked

about . . ." Once again his eyes drifted to the ceiling. "Uh . . ."

"Exactly."

His gaze sharpened. "Jessie, this Smitherton partnership is crucial to me. I've worked hard for it. It's all I want. I don't have time for a . . ."

Jessie raised a brow. "Relationship?"

Martin remained silent.

"Exactly," Jessie said softly. She reached down and picked up his pants from a nearby chair, holding them out to him. "I think you'd better go now."

"I . . . I didn't quite mean it like that."

"Yes, you did. It's just not working, Martin. We both want different things."

Martin took his pants from her. "All right." He hurriedly got into his slacks and moved toward the door. In the doorway, he paused and turned to face her. "I'll come get the rest of my stuff next Sunday night, okay?"

"Sure."

"Jess . . . I'm sorry. I didn't mean—"

"It's okay, Martin. Good-bye."

He nodded his head, then turned away.

Jessie remained where she was until she heard the click of the lock on the front door. She realized belatedly that she should have asked him to leave his keys. Well, she'd get them when he came to pick up his few belongings.

She turned and walked around the room, blowing out each candle until only the dim light from the moon filtered through the drawn curtains to brighten the room. Once again, she walked to the window and parted the drapes. She peered out into the backyard, gazing in the direction of the gazebo—the gazebo where she'd thought Martin stood watching as she'd stripped and stroked her body, her skin tingling, her excitement growing as she imagined Martin's reaction, his erection, as he'd watched. And when she'd brushed Teddy against her body, imagining it was Martin . . .

She reached down and picked up Teddy, then leaned against the window frame.

"But it wasn't Martin, was it?" she asked.

Jessie stared into the bear's glassy brown eyes and moved his head side-to-side.

"And a mere stranger had made me feel better than Martin ever had, hadn't he?"

Her fingers forced Teddy's head up and down.

God, it'd felt so good—and Nick hadn't really touched her. No caresses, no kisses. He'd gone straight to her pussy without foreplay and she'd been hot. Hotter than she'd ever been. So hot that she'd had a hard time believing it was Martin.

At the time, little did she know she was right. Now, she was glad it wasn't Martin.

She hugged Teddy to her chest and turned her attention to the ocean.

Well, it was over with Martin. He was history.

She frowned. Wasn't this the point where the tears were supposed to course down her cheeks? The point where she was supposed to bang her head against the windowpane and shriek, *Oh, Martin!*

Jessie did a quick inventory of her feelings and her frown deepened.

Nothing.

She felt nothing, other than a sense of relief that she now had the whole closet to herself, that the top shelf of the medicine cabinet would once again contain her nail polish collection.

Absolutely nothing.

Except the lingering synapses of lust for a stranger. A stranger that she would never see again.

The thought made her wonder what he had been doing at the vacant house in the first place. She should've asked him. But, the roar of sexual feelings had deafened all rational thought.

Jessie sighed and turned towards the bed, taking off her robe as she went. She set Teddy down, slipped under the covers, and stared at the ceiling. She waited, again, for the loss of Martin to hit her, to suddenly wrap itself around her heart like a vise . . .

Instead, as she shifted her position in the bed, the feel of the silky sheets brushing her skin became the invisible fingers of a brown-eyed stranger, brushing her thighs and caressing her nipples. Jessie moaned softly and slid her hands under the covers, imagining that he—that *Nick*—was back in the bed with her.

She cupped her breasts, feeling his hands squeeze them.

She drew light circles against her flesh, feeling his tongue instead of her fingers.

"Suck my nipples," she whispered.

Her fingers, tugging on her nipples, were Nick's teeth.

The palm of her hands, rolling her nipples, became his tongue.

"Yes," she said, pressing her thighs together tightly, and thrusting her hips upward, then downward.

"Open your legs," Nick said.

Jessie uncrossed her ankles and spread her legs. She continued rolling the palm of her hands against her nipples.

His tongue continued licking her nipple.

Her hips continued fucking the air.

He stopped.

"No . . ."

"What do you want?" Nick whispered.

She slid her palms down her body, over her stomach, and down her hips.

He slid his hands down her body.

She ran her fingers along her thighs.

Nick stroked the sensitive skin of her inner thighs with the pad of his finger, before moving inward, lightly caressing her naked lips.

She bucked her hips.

"What do you want?" He breathed the words in her ear, now on top of her, with his fingers between their bodies. He slipped a finger between her needy lips and stroked.

Jessie arched her back, sucking in jerky breaths. "Yessss . . ."

Her fingers strummed her clit.

He rubbed her clit faster and harder. "What do you want?"

She spread her legs wider and ground her hips faster. "I want you . . . to . . . fuck me."

The F word, something she never said to a lover, caused her heart to skitter in her chest and her finger to dip inside her pussy, moving in and out and around and around.

Nick thrust into her hard and fast.

Jessie gasped at the shock of his entry. The heat searing her, spreading over every inch of her flesh, was no longer caused by her fingers.

His cock ignited her nerve endings and sparked her flesh.

Sensation was building . . . building . . . building . .

.

"Please . . . Oh, I want it. Need it. Now."

Her finger flew over her clit.

His cock slammed into her.

Her hips jerked up and down, meeting him, forcing him to go faster.

"Shit," he said as he drove into her, seconds before his cock pulsed inside her pussy and his body quaked.

Spasms slammed through her body and waves of heat collided inside her. Her fingers slowed, then stopped.

"Thank you, Nick," she said when the last quiver had died. As she drifted off to sleep, her heart felt as light as cotton candy and her body felt as limp as the sheet draped over her.

6

Coffee cup in hand, Jessie crossed the porch and bent down to retrieve the *Narragansett Gazette*. Standing, she sipped her coffee and glanced at the paper. But, as she'd done for the past week, she found her thoughts drifting. Instead of seeing photos of the mayoral candidates, images of Nick flashed through her brain—of his dark head between her legs, of his tongue shooting spears of need over her stomach and to her breasts, making her body tremble. Her thighs had clenched with the urge to hold him to her, pull him closer, and prevent him from stopping.

Jessie was obsessed by Nick, by what he'd made her feel.

It felt like a spigot had been turned on. Decadent thoughts and feelings roiled around inside her, building and building, only to be blocked from release. Masturbation wasn't cutting it; she wasn't a one-night-stand kind of woman; and the kicker, she hadn't once thought of Martin, let alone missed him.

When you realize Martin can't give you what you need, let

me know

Who the hell was Nick? Why had he been in the backyard that night?

And most importantly, was he as good with his cock as his tongue and hands promised?

Shaking her head in disgust, she turned to make her way back into the house. The sudden roar of a car engine caused her to jerk around, which in turn caused hot java to slosh against her skin. But she barely noticed, her ears tuned in to a sound reminiscent of last week.

Her gaze latched on to the gleaming black Porsche Boxster pulling up into the front driveway of the house next door.

The driver's side door opened and closed.

A brown-haired man got out. He was dressed in jeans that hugged lean hips and a black T-shirt that couldn't hide his muscular shoulders.

Jessie blinked.

Dark glasses hid his eyes, but she'd be willing to bet they were brown. Her breath caught in her throat as he faced her dead-on.

Jessie forced regular breaths, attempting to stave off a bout of hyperventilation.

It was *him*.

His lips curved slightly, he nodded at her, and . . .

Jessie froze, willing him to step forward and walk over to her.

Instead, he turned away.

Disappointment flared deep in her stomach. She continued to stare, unable to look away, admiring the way the jeans hugged Nick's ass as he walked to the sign staked in the ground near the mailbox. He removed the "For Sale" portion of the sign.

"My new neighbor . . .?" she whispered.

Did that breathy voice just come out of her?

Oh. My. God.

Her heart did a somersault in her chest at the possibility that this exquisitely sculpted hunk might be her new neighbor.

Her pulse sang.

He wasn't a pervert, skulking around neighborhoods at night. He'd been in the yard because he'd bought the house. Well, he could be a home owning pervert but—

Wait a minute. What if . . .

Nick continued to stand at the foot of the driveway, staring at the street as if waiting for someone.

. . . What if he was waiting for an SUV filled with a smiling wife and a vanload of energetic children?

Her heart took a nosedive for her stomach. She pulled her robe tighter around her and closed her eyes.

Please don't let a woman drive up. Surely Nick wouldn't have hinted at his abilities to satisfy her carnal needs if—Hell, forget hinted at. Surely he wouldn't lick and nibble her starving flesh if he was married with a family.

In this day and age, yes, he very well would.

Jessie opened her eyes.

Nick lifted a hand . . .

Jessie held her breath.

. . . to flag a moving truck.

The breath exploded from her lungs. Her heart returned to her chest. As Nick turned and walked up the driveway, he looked her way.

Long and hard.

Maybe images of being in her bed flitted through his brain. Maybe, behind those dark lenses, he was remembering her scent and taste and wanting more.

On impulse, Jessie lifted a hand and waved.

Once again, Nick nodded. After opening the garage, he disappeared inside.

Men in orange T-shirts and jeans unloaded the truck.

Jessie remained motionless, thinking. Okay, so Nick's response wasn't the most enthusiastic one she'd ever encountered. Especially after their last interaction. But, on the other hand, he had told her to come to him when she realized Martin couldn't give her what she needed.

Smiling, Jessie turned and scurried into the house.

Well, come to him she would, indeed.

7

Jessie mounted the last step and glanced inside the big bay window. Boxes seemed to cover every available inch of the living room, including the leather sofa and matching chair.

Her breath caught in her throat as her eyes rested on the man kneeling on the hardwood floor in front of the expensive entertainment center. Gone was the black T-shirt, giving her an excellent view of the masculine back and muscles that rippled as he fiddled with, well, whatever he was fiddling with.

He could be plucking strands of lint from between the knobs of the stereo for all she cared. All that interested her at the moment was the play of his deltoids as he moved, the flawless skin that looked as smooth as marble, the—

Suddenly, he stood, jerking her out of her trance.

She turned away and hurried to the door before he could turn around and catch her gaping at him. She tugged nervously on the hem of her dress. She was a novice at seduction.

What if he was no longer interested in her? What if she couldn't seduce him?

Take charge
Be bold.
Do it.
Go sin.

Jessie rang the bell. As she waited for him to answer, she fluffed the tissue paper lining the basket she carried and straightened the bow on the handle.

A few seconds later, the door opened and she got a frontal view of his lust-provoking chest. Well, what little she could see out of the corner of her eyes. After all, staring and drooling at his chest would spoil the cool, in-control image she was shooting for.

She willed her gaze to remain fixed on his face, to not inch downward and explore the light coating of hair that dusted his chest, to not see if his jeans molded his hips like she suspected they did. Instead, she stared directly into his eyes. Eyes that were dark brown, just as she'd remembered, but without the warmth she'd seen when he'd looked up at her from between her legs.

Today, his eyes seemed to regard her politely.

Oh, God. Had he changed his mind?

Jessie gave him what she hoped was a dazzling smile—friendly, sexy, and interested all in one. "Hi. Since it looks like we're going to be neighbors, I wanted to welcome you to the neighborhood and introduce myself . . ."

She changed the tone of her voice, going for what she hoped was a throaty purr.

". . . properly. I'm Jessie Anderson."

She stuck out her hand.

His gaze flicked from her eyes to her hand, before

once again returning to her face. The trip seemed to have changed his eye color from a soft brown to mocha.

Ahh, it looked like he was definitely warming up.

Finally, he grasped her hand, his strong, lean fingers completely engulfing her own. Once again, her body registered that these were *not* the pampered hands of a man who created spreadsheets all day, but rather, the functional hands of a man who used them.

A thrill shot through her at the slight roughness.

A pang of disappointment whizzed through her when he dropped her hand.

Jessie held the basket out to him. "Well, then . . . welcome to the neighborhood."

His eyes flicked to the basket, which he regarded with the same intensity as he'd regarded her fingers. After a few seconds, he took it from her.

"Thank you," he said.

Jessie smiled. "You're welcome."

She watched him rake a hand through his hair as he uttered a frustrated sigh. "Come in. We need to talk."

Talk?

Jessie frowned. Talking was not exactly what she had in mind. And since every man she'd ever known looked forward to serious conversation about as much as they relished having their chest hairs plucked with tweezers, "we need to talk" did not bode well.

She stood where she was.

He moved to the side.

With a shrug, she followed him into the house.

8

Nick knew that the last thing in the world he should do was invite Jessie into his house. Each morning, for the last seven days, he'd woken up with a hard-on and the memory of her juices teasing his taste buds.

He'd told her to contact him when she'd gotten rid of Martin.

Instead, she stood in front of him as a delegate from the Neighborhood Welcome Committee.

Her tousled black hair called to his fingers, her full lips glistened, begging him to devour their ripeness. His eyes took in every centimeter of her curvy body—which the simple dress erotically accentuated—to her painted toenails. Fire-engine red. He wanted to take each toe in his hands, gently spread them apart and suck until—

This was exactly the reason why he should have accepted her cookies, slammed the door behind her, and returned to tuning his amps.

Jessie made him feel lust when he didn't want to

feel anything. He *couldn't* feel anything.

She was another man's woman.

His lips twisted—*Martin's* woman. Despite the fact that Martin was a dud in bed—Nick knew this because he'd barely gotten started when her body had quaked and quivered in his hands—he was not going to commit another wrong and finish what he'd started.

Even though his cock wanted to.

He turned and led the way to the kitchen, wanting to put some physical distance between her tempting body and his over-stimulated cock. Pushing aside a cardboard box of dishes sitting on the countertop, he sat the basket beside the box.

"I hope you have a sweet tooth. I made them myself."

Great. Not only did she taste good, she could bake. He ignored the goodies in the basket, looking at her instead. Plump lips. Plump breasts. Round hips. Goodies much more succulent than those resting between a bunch of twigs.

Damn.

"Look, we need to talk," he said.

"Let's have a snack first."

Images of his last "snack" with her zoomed through his mind—legs caressing his cheeks while his tongue had tasted her wetness, sampling the musky flavor that made him crave more.

He blinked. "Snack?"

"The basket," she prompted, her tone slightly amused, her bright eyes seemingly innocent.

Nick felt his face grow warm. He had to get these thoughts out of his mind. Shit, one would think he was starved for sex by the way he was acting—which was far from the truth. He had an active—albeit empty—sex life. But there was something about the dichotomy—the sexy vixen at odds with the girl-next-door freshness—that threw him off balance.

He snorted inwardly. *She is the girl next door.*

Okay. Food. Food would help him focus. Nick peered inside the basket and parted the tissue paper. He stared at the contents.

His cock twitched.

She laughed. A throaty, husky sound that belonged in the bedroom.

"I know they're a little juvenile, but I love bears," she said.

Nick lifted one of the bear cookies from the basket, noting the two-piece bathing suit that had been painted in red icing. Visions of just how much she loved bears flitted through his mind, of last week's bear getting to lick and lave the body he'd been denied, the sweet wetness he'd barely tasted. Pushing those images from his mind, he raised his gaze to Jessie's.

Merriment, with a hint of mischief, sparkled in her brown eyes.

Against his will, his gaze once again flicked over the "v" of her top. In his mind he stripped it from her body, seeing her breasts teasing him in the sheer red lingerie, breasts that the stuffed bear had "kissed." Breasts that he had kissed. Until she'd discovered he wasn't Martin.

His jaw tightened. He dropped the bear in the basket and pushed it away, returning his gaze to hers. "Look, I'm sorry about last week. What I did was wrong—"

"It didn't feel wrong," purred the sexy vixen.

He ignored the silky tone and the seductive smile curving her lips, instead focusing on the words he had to say. "Well, it *was* wrong and I—"

"Do you have anything to drink?"

What the hell was going on here? He was trying to talk and she wanted something to drink?

Nick frowned.

Jessie's shrug seemed apologetic. "I'm thirsty."

"Uh, tap water and maybe a bottle of wine. Somewhere."

"Wine sounds good."

Wine was the nectar of seduction. Not the drinking of the wine, but rather, watching Jessie's lips brush the rim of the glass instead of his lips or his neck or . . . his cock.

Wine sounded *really* good.

Enough of this. They were going to talk.

"Where's Martin?" His voice was harsher than he'd planned.

Jessie drew back. "Martin?"

Her tongue darted out, drawing his eyes to its movement as the pink flesh slid over the corner of her lip before hiding in her mouth. The gesture seemed to be made out of nervousness, not eroticism, but he still found the movement sensual. He wanted to nibble the moist flesh and suckle the soft tongue before thrusting into its wet hiding place.

"Um . . . Martin's gone."

Thoughts of Sandy came unbidden to his mind. When he'd caught up with the lies and called her on them, she'd shrugged and said, "Those men don't mean anything to me, Nicky. I love *you.*" Was Jessie planning to dupe Martin and entice Nick to become one of the men who "didn't mean anything" to her?

"So you thought you'd come over here and 'play'?" While the cat was away and all that.

She grinned. "Yeah."

His jaw clenched. It shouldn't bother him, but it did. He'd wanted to believe that she was different, that the girl-next-door freshness meant goodness that went beyond the surface. But, while he'd been feeling remorse for his actions, she'd been intent on compounding the wrong.

Well, it doesn't bother your cock. Go ahead and "play" with her.

Nick returned his attention to Jessie.

Her smile disappeared. Her gaze became uncertain seconds before understanding seemed to dawn. "Oh. I meant Martin's *gone,* as in out of my life. I broke up with him."

Nick's anger subsided. Relief took its place. Jessie's news flash changed things—if it was true, that is. "Why?"

She frowned. "Does it really matter why?"

Yes, it mattered. Especially if Martin didn't realize it was over and was going to come banging on his door.

He shrugged. "Last week, you were trying to seduce him. This week, you're seducing me."

"Am I? Seducing you?"

Hell, yeah. Her lidded eyes and plump lips sent another rush of blood to his groin.

He shifted, trying to relieve a bit of pressure.

"Didn't you tell me to call you when I realized that Martin couldn't give me what I needed? Well . . ." She licked her lower lip. ". . . I'm calling you."

Thank you, God. She was not representing the Neighborhood Welcome Committee.

Her words were a dream come true. A *wet* dream come true. She wanted him. She was available. She was accessible. Hell, she lived next door—

Ah, shit. He hadn't been thinking with the big head when he'd told her to come to him. The fact was that they were neighbors and, after the sex was gone, they'd still be neighbors. The needs he'd been referring to were strictly the physical, you-come-I-come kind of needs. Nothing more.

He'd said the words because they'd popped into his mind—and, if he were honest, his ego had gotten the better of him. He'd been feeling superior, filled with lust and bravado because he'd been satisfying her in ways Martin never had. He'd figured she'd eventually dump the inept Martin, but he'd never thought she'd do it this soon.

Had she broken up with Martin because of what he'd said? Was she looking for a relationship?

Damn. He hadn't been *thinking* at all.

"Is there a problem?" she asked.

Hell, no. No problem here, his cock urged.

He raised a brow. "Rebounding?"

She laughed.

He waited.

"No," she said after the laughter died. "I'm not rebounding. To rebound, there has to be something to rebound from. Martin and I were over long before you . . . showed up. That night was an irrational attempt to postpone the inevitable. Today is a rational attempt to have some fun."

Sounds good to me. "You just want fun?"

"Yes." She looked him straight in the eyes.

Okay. She wanted him. She wanted sex. She didn't want the big R—a relationship.

His conscience was happy.

"So . . . are you going to satisfy my . . ." Her tongue made another appearance between her lips. ". . . thirst."

"Are you sure you're thirsty?"

Her gaze dropped, seemingly focused on his mouth. Her smile slipped. Her eyes darkened.

His cock lengthened.

"Oh, yes. Very thirsty," she said.

Her sultry purr suddenly left his throat parched. He was very thirsty, too.

Let the thirst-quenching begin.

"Well, then . . ." Nick smiled and turned, rummaging through a nearby box. He was going to drag this out, switch the roles, and leave her off balance. "Voila," he said, his hand circling the desired item. "Merlot. Red wine goes with red dishes." He sat the bottle on the countertop with a flourish.

Jessie burst out laughing. No braying sound to this laugh. Rather, a sultry purr that penetrated his skin and circulated through his blood stream, raising his temperature by ten degrees.

Or, was that twenty?

He ignored its effect.

For the moment.

She picked up a bear clad in red boxer shorts. "Then I'm glad I brought the red dish."

"Me, too." Only he wasn't talking about red bear cookies. Instead, he was imagining her body as he'd last seen it, blazing hot underneath the red robe, nipples hard and begging to be tasted.

She blushed, her lowered gaze implying that she'd read his mind.

He grinned. "Make yourself at home while I look

for glasses." His gaze scanned the stacks of boxes. "This may take a while," he finished wryly.

He watched her turn and stroll towards the living room, his need no longer masked as he stared at her ass, seeing the firm cheeks she'd cupped between her fingers.

He forced the enticing picture out of his mind and turned his attention back to the task at hand. He tore open a second box and prayed that he'd find glasses inside. God must've been listening, for not only were there glasses, but a corkscrew as well. He whispered a thanks as he swept the wine, corkscrew, glasses, and basket from the counter, then grabbed a roll of paper towels and headed for the living room.

His eyes immediately went to Jessie as she squatted in front of the CD rack.

"You have quite a CD collection," she said over her shoulder.

He watched a red-tipped nail, at odds with her current Susie Homemaker image, lightly skip over the CDs.

"Luther Vandross, Kenny G, Uncle Kracker . . ." she recited, standing.

He placed everything on the coffee table and joined her in front of the CD stand. He smiled and stopped behind her, invading her space. "Yeah, I like a little bit of everything." His breath stirred her hair.

Did she shrug or was that a shiver?

Reaching around her, he intentionally brushed her arm as he reached for a CD. The buzz that went through him momentarily distracted him. Jessie jumped, obviously affected just as he had been.

Ahhh. The sexy siren wasn't as calm and collected as she pretended to be. So, his breath must've caused a shiver.

He smiled and resumed his search, stopping at the Fourplay CD. "Have you heard this one before?"

"No. Fourplay? What is it?" she asked.

The tremor in her voice pleased him. More than pleased him. Excited him. He fought the urge to slip his hands under her skirt and around her waist, before pulling her hips back and rubbing her ass against his cock.

Instead, he reached around her and opened the CD changer. Their bare arms once again brushed, sending another jolt through him.

"Let me show you," he whispered in her ear.

9

Jessie forced her breathing to remain even, normal, as Nick reached around her. The heat from his chest seemed to burn her back through her thin cotton top. And he wasn't even touching her. She imagined what she'd feel if she leaned back a fraction of an inch, leaning into the hardness of his chest.

And she knew it would be hard. She could tell by the way his muscles flexed when he moved. The same muscles that she'd been trying to ignore since she'd walked through the door.

She jumped when his arm touched hers again as he opened the CD changer. What was wrong with her? The man had just barely brushed against her and she wanted to grab his arms and grind her body along the hard length of him. She had to get her body under control. Otherwise, her plan to seduce him—to drive *him* wild—would end in embarrassment.

She wanted to appear sexy and seductive, not desperate.

With a start, she realized he'd been talking to her.

"I'm sorry. What did you say? I . . . was listening to this CD."

His laugh rumbled behind her. Deep. Low. Sexy. "I asked you what you thought of the music."

Jessie tuned in to the music, listening for the first time, trying to ignore Nick's hips that were mere inches away. A male voice crooned some ballad about waiting for love. His problems sounded trivial to her, compared to the battle of desire going on inside her.

She struggled to come up with something seductive.

"It's aptly named," she said, dropping her voice to a husky rasp. "The music pulses with energy that caresses the skin and strokes the soul, making the body want to move in . . . hard . . . slow . . . movements . . ."

Did she hear him draw a shaky breath?

"Great description." His voice was hoarse.

Eureka!

Jessie smiled as he stepped away from her. Maybe she was better at seduction than she thought.

She turned around and faced Nick.

"Have a seat," he said as he moved a box out of the way.

As she sat down on the couch, she watched him work the cork out of the bottle and sink into the leather chair opposite her.

Damn.

She'd hoped he'd take a seat next to her. Kind of hard to run her fingers along his arm or down his chest from ten feet away.

Time to come up with plan B.

While he reached for a cookie, her eyes roamed greedily over his chest, down to where the waistband of his jeans met his tight abdomen. Mingled with her blatant lust was a stab of envy. It wasn't fair that he could lean over without displaying a trace of flab. She had to spend hours on the Lifecycle for every ounce of muscle she possessed.

She averted her eyes hastily as he leaned back in his chair, long legs sprawled out in front of him, carelessly parted in a "v."

He munched on a cookie, then said, "Mmmmm. These are great. I think I've acquired a love of bears as well."

The slight emphasis on the word "bears" made Jessie wonder if he was referring to Teddy, the way she had slid the stuffed bear across her abdomen and over her pussy.

Her face felt warm, pleasantly warm.

She leaned back against the couch and stretched.

Nick's gaze dropped to her breasts.

Jessie smiled. "I'm glad you like my bears." She lowered her hands, moving one to her breast, tracing the edge of her top with a fingertip. "So what should we do next, Nick? Get to know each other?"

Nick's smile seduced while his eyes followed the movement of her fingertip. "Two people getting to know each other is always good."

She traced her cleavage.

Nick licked his lips.

"Okay . . ."

She slid her fingers under her top, caressing her flesh, nearing her nipple.

". . . What brings you to Narragansett?"

"I'm buying a commercial building in Providence . . . Narragansett is close. This is a great house . . ." He sounded distracted.

Jessie forced her eyes away from his, ignoring the heat in his gaze, letting her gaze circle the room instead.

She smiled. "Yes, this is a great house. It's got great windows." She pointed to the bay window she'd observed him through earlier. "That one is perfect for . . . entertaining."

She turned back to Nick. He held the wineglass by the stem, idly swirling the red wine, looking as if his mind was elsewhere. And, if she judged the smoky gleam in his eyes correctly, his mind was definitely elsewhere.

Probably rolling around in the gutter with hers.

His lips quirked and he inclined his head slightly. "Is that what you came over here for? To entertain me?"

"No. I did not come over to entertain, Nick."

He took a sip of wine.

She watched his mouth as he drank the wine. His mouth. Her body flooded with remembrance. She wanted his mouth back—on her, not on some stupid wineglass.

Jessie picked up a bear cookie with polka-dot boxers. She sucked lightly on the bear's leg.

Nick's smile slipped.

"I came over to play, Nick . . ." She removed the cookie from her mouth, licking the bear instead, letting her tongue outline the foot and leg, stopping at the "v" between its legs.

Nick's gaze was riveted on her mouth.

Jessie's gaze was riveted on his mouth, to the tongue that peeked out between his lips as he licked them lightly.

She swallowed hard.

"What game did you have in mind?" he asked.

Her mind scrambled to think, for she hadn't been *thinking* of anything. Instead, she'd been *feeling—feeling* heat begin to spread through her body at the sight of the sexual haze that seemed to cloud his gaze. And, as the heat spread, growing hotter, traveling faster, the harder it became to think of something.

No, playing games was the last thing that had been on her mind when she'd showed up on his doorstep. And, now, the only game she wanted to play, was one that involved the two of them naked, their bodies touching, their hands stroking, satisfying the ache that was growing stronger and stronger within her—

Ache . . . Games . . .

Jessie bit off the bear's leg and smiled. "Doctor."

"Huh?"

Apparently, she wasn't the only one having trouble thinking.

Nick raised his gaze from her lips to her eyes, and blinked, as if trying to focus.

"I came over to play 'Doctor.'"

Lightbulbs did not appear to be going off behind his eyes. In fact, his eyes had that hooded look that implied his thoughts were sexual, still on the action of her lips on the bear cookie, possibly imagining her lips on him, kissing, nibbling, joined by the swirl of her tongue and—

Her breath caught in her throat. She forced it out lightly. "Surely you played 'Doctor' when you were a kid?"

"No."

"Well. That seems positively un-American."

"I guess I'm deprived." His smile was sly. "So un-deprive me. I'm ready to play."

He reached for another cookie. Jessie watched his teeth encircle the bikini-clad bear, taking an almost delicate bite.

That was odd. There was nothing about Nick that was dainty or delicate. Then she noticed where he'd taken the bite.

He'd eaten the crotch.

Her eyes snapped to his, catching the devilish glint behind the sexy stare.

"Show me," he said softly.

10

Heat rushed to her pussy at the thought of showing Nick how to play "Doctor." Jessie ignored her body's response, determined to drag things out, to tease Nick—and herself. Striving to remain as nonchalant as he appeared to be, she picked up the wineglass.

"I'm the doctor and you're the patient. First, we'll need . . ."

She ran her fingertip lightly around the rim before dipping it into the dark liquid. Lifting her wine-coated finger to her lips, her tongue darting out, lightly licking the tip, before suckling it with a kiss-like movement. All the while, she stared directly into Nick's eyes, watching his eyes darken as he watched her.

". . . medicine."

She made a big production of sipping the wine, raising the glass slowly to her lips, taking a leisurely sip, letting it linger in her mouth just a bit, before swallowing noticeably.

Nick watched the intoxicating liquid slide down her throat, with what appeared to be envy.

She smiled and tilted the glass. "Yes, I think that this will do." She stood. "Next, we'll need an examining table."

Nick popped up from the chair and rushed to the dining room, nearly flinging the boxes off the table.

When the table was cleared, he turned to her, his expression eager. "Will this do?"

She hid a grin. "Yes. Now you need to hop up on the table and lie down."

He swung himself up and lay on his back, near the edge.

Jessie stepped forward, stopping next to him and setting the glass on the tabletop. "Now, I need to examine you, see if you have any hurts that I can fix."

"Doctor, I'm in great pain."

She met his gaze. Anticipation, not pain, shone in his eyes, proving him to be a lousy actor.

Jessie's lips twitched. "Yes, I can see that." She ran her fingers over his shoulders. "I bet you hurt here . . ." She trailed her fingertips over his chest, circling his areola, pinching his nipples.

He inhaled sharply. "Yes."

". . . and here . . ." She trailed her fingers over his abdomen.

His stomach rippled. "Yes."

"You hurt from all that heavy lifting you did today."

"Yes."

She retraced the path of her fingers. "Kisses always make the pain a little less."

"That might make the pain a little worse," he said, his gaze locked on the movement of her hand.

Jessie smiled. "Sometimes it has to hurt before it gets better. About the pain here . . ." She leaned forward and placed her lips against his collarbone, kissing and tracing it with her tongue, before moving upward. She sucked and licked the muscle that ran from his neck to his shoulder.

Nick moved his head to the side, giving her better access.

"Feel better?" she asked.

"No," he said between gritted teeth.

While suckling his neck, she let her hands wander over his chest, palms caressing his pecs. She felt his nipples turn into hard nubs under her flesh.

He inhaled sharply.

"Feel better now?"

Nick remained silent.

She trailed her tongue over his chest, flicking his nipples, before moving down to his abdomen.

His stomach quivered.

She dipped her fingers under the waistband of his jeans, her palm resting on his cock. "Hmmm . . . I notice a bit of swelling here."

She raised her head from his stomach and traced his waist with her fingertips.

His cock traced his zipper.

"It's very swollen," he said.

"Yes. And it looks very, very painful," she said throatily.

"It is." His voice was hoarse. "I need release."

She gave him a disapproving stare. "Release, Mr. Ralston?"

"Oh . . . Uh . . . I meant, relief. I need relief."

Judging by the way his voice cracked, he did sound like a man in need. And judging by the way his eyes blazed, he looked like a man in dire need of what she could give him.

"Yes, you do," she said.

Using both hands, Jessie unbuttoned the top button on his jeans. "I'm going to have to take off your jeans to get a closer look at your condition, Mr. Ralston. Do you mind?"

"No. Please."

"I must warn you. We ran out of hospital gowns."

"That's fine, that's fine. I just need—"

"Relief. I understand, Mr. Ralston."

She unzipped his jeans, her eyes glued to the ever-growing bulge beneath her touch.

Ever helpful, Nick lifted his hips.

Jessie tugged the jeans over them, then hooked her fingers in the sides of his briefs and repeated the downward motion.

"Why, Mr. Ralston, I don't believe I've met a patient so eager to assist in—"

As his cock cleared the cotton, the words died in her throat and her heart slammed in her chest.

"Wow," she breathed.

Despite the male obsession with size, she'd never paid much attention to it, believing that how a man used his cock—not the size of it—was what mattered.

It was easy to disregard size when she'd never had to consider it before. But looking at the cock pointing towards Nick's navel, she decided that maybe she'd discounted size prematurely. For size gave a woman additional options—if the man didn't know what to do with it, the woman did. After all, she was a master with her dildo, and Nick seemed to be at least as big.

But she'd be willing to bet he'd know what to do with his natural . . . gift. Surely someone with such skill with his mouth and tongue—

"Is there a problem, Doctor?"

"Ooooh, no—no problem here." She sounded breathless.

Nick's chuckle was strained.

Jessie continued pulling downward, until his underwear joined his jeans around his ankles.

"Yes, yes, I can see why you were in pain. There appears to be extreme rigidity . . ." She wrapped her hand around his cock.

The breath hissed out of him.

"Did that hurt?"

"Oh, yeah."

Oh, God. He felt so good in her hand. His skin was so smooth, his cock was so hard. She wanted to climb onto the table and straddle his hips and—

"Is there a cure?" His tone was urgent.

"I . . . I think s-so." Her voice trembled. Jessie cleared the lust from her throat. "We're going to have to try multiple treatments."

"Okay."

"First, we're going to try a . . . therapeutic massage." She moved her hand up his shaft.

Nick moaned.

She stopped. "Is that too painful, Mr. Ralston?"

"No." His hand gripped hers, moving it down his cock.

She jerked her hand away. "I am the doctor and you are the patient. Do I have to buckle your hands down onto the examining table?" Her attempt to be stern failed.

She sounded aroused.

He let his hands fall to the side. "Sorry, Doctor." His attempt at contrition failed.

He sounded impatient.

Jessie pressed her lips together to contain her smile. Once again, she wrapped her hand around his cock. She moved it down to the base, her wrist touching his balls.

He thrust his hips up.

She moved her hand up, burying the head of his cock in her palm.

He yanked his hips down.

His movement was frantic, inciting her passion, igniting her need. Her breathing was ragged.

"Y-you seem to be c-crazed by pain. I think you need a painkiller. Open your m-mouth."

He did as instructed.

Her hand shook as she reached for the glass. She dipped her forefinger into the wine and touched his tongue.

He licked her finger, swirling his tongue around the tip and up the sides, before closing his lips around it. His mouth felt hot and moist.

He sucked and licked.

Jessie gasped. God, the man was good with his mouth.

His cock fucked her hand.

His mouth fucked her finger.

Jessie's body thrummed with need.

Suddenly, Nick turned his head to the side, dislodging her finger, and gripped her hands, stilling her stroking of his cock. "No," he said between gritted teeth.

Jessie stilled.

Nick stilled.

His ragged breathing filled the air. "You're a lousy doctor," he said finally. "My pain is worse than when you started."

Jessie feigned a hurt expression. "Well, if you feel that way . . ." She let go of his cock and slid her hands from under his, then drew back, intent on moving away.

Nick sat up and swung his legs to the side of the table. He kicked his jeans and briefs from around his ankles and stood. Putting his hands on her thighs, he pulled her to him. His hands caressed her skin, making their way under the hem of her skirt.

Nick's breath hissed out of him, ending on a curse. "You aren't wearing panties?"

"A doctor comes prepared for action."

Nick made a strangled sound in the back of his throat. His hand moved to the nape of her neck, pulling her forward, bringing her mouth to his.

As her lips touched his, all thoughts of their game went out of her mind. His lips were so soft. Her mouth parted under his and she strained forward, coaxing them wider with her tongue, desperate for a taste. Her heart doubled its beat, her breathing accelerated. Slipping her hand to the base of his neck, she pulled his head closer. Slanting her head, she took the kiss deeper.

Nick's hands massaged and stroked her shoulders, before moving down her back. His other hand joined the action. Up and down, his hands moved restlessly over her.

Nick broke the kiss, his breath rasping in his throat.

Jessie opened her eyes—when had she closed them?—in time to see his head lower, in time to feel his lips on her throat. He kissed, inhaling at the same time, creating a cooling sensation that heated her skin.

Jessie shivered.

"You seem to have pain, too," he whispered against her neck, the warm air heating her flesh just as the cool air had done. He trailed his tongue along her shoulder, tracing the path her fingers had made when she'd pointed out his pain, going lower, across the swell of her breasts accessible above the neckline of her top.

"N-no, I'm fine," she lied, remembering the game, struggling to get it back on track, despite the very real "pain" inflamed by his tongue.

She drew back.

He pulled her forward, and bent down, his mouth capturing a nipple through the cloth.

"Oh!" she cried.

His mouth suckled.

Sensation careened through her body, sparked by the simple action of his moist mouth searing her through the thin material, his firm hands massaging her tense body.

Jessie pulled her chest back, wanting him to pull the cotton away from her skin and take her flesh in his mouth. She pressed her hips forward and upward, using the friction to quell some of the need surging through her.

Nick tightened his grip on her hips and pivoted. The next thing she knew, Jessie found herself sitting on the table. "What are you doing?"

His hands strummed her back, seeking, searching, finding her zipper on the back of her top. He pulled it down. "Putting you on the examining table."

"The doctor belongs on the other side of the table."

He slid the straps of her top over her shoulders

and off her hands. The halter top pooled around her waist. Her nipples instantly hardened under his stare.

Nick lifted his gaze to hers. His eyes blazed with want. His lips curved into a smile. "I think I understand how this game works. I'm the doctor now."

11

Before Jessie could respond, his mouth returned to her breast, his flesh touching her flesh, just as she'd tried to urge him to do in the living room.

"Is that where it hurts?" he asked, his voice muffled by the nipple he teased with his tongue.

Jessie moaned and her hands tightened on his shoulders. This time, her hold on him wasn't for fear of falling but, rather, for fear that he'd move away, that he'd stop swirling his tongue, which would put an end to the delicious tingles sparking from her chest, dipping into her stomach, dropping lower to the lips swollen with want.

Her thighs guided him closer.

He leaned forward and while his mouth continued teasing her breasts, his body forced her backward.

Jessie removed her hands from Nick's shoulders and used her elbows to ease her descent onto the tabletop.

The glass tabletop felt hard and cold under her back. Nick's tongue felt soft and hot against her skin.

She placed her hands to his head, pressing him closer, guiding him to the left, then right, coercing him to apply more pressure.

"Is this where it hurts?" he repeated, warming her nipple with his breath.

She gasped and arched her back, pushing her nipple deeper into his throat. "Yes, it hurts there. But it really hurts. . ." She reached in her skirt pocket and removed a condom, holding it out to him.

"Ah, I see." He tore the packet open and put it on, then grabbed her hips and pulled her down to the edge of the table. "It really hurts *here*." His cock nudged her pussy.

"Oh, yes!" She gripped his hips tightly with her thighs. His cock nestled against her pussy.

She groaned.

He moaned.

"You need to make it better . . . now!" She pressed forward for emphasis.

While his mouth worked its magic on her skin—from one nipple to the next, laving and tasting, to her throat, past her shoulder, finally returning to her mouth—his fingers slid between their bodies, guiding what she wanted most to where she most wanted it.

His cock hovered inside her pussy lips. "Is this what you wanted?"

Jessie thrust her hips forward, pushing him inside her.

He cursed.

She cried.

His hips pumped.

Her hands gripped, pulling him closer, greedy for more—more flesh against flesh, more flesh inside flesh, more feeling, more sensation. Awe and desire swirled inside her. Awe because while Nick had barely fondled her body, he'd ignited her passion. His words, the intensity of his focus—as if she where the only woman who mattered—the tease of his touch, served as mental foreplay, which inflamed her body with physical want.

Martin's touch had been functional, an act performed seemingly because it was required.

Nick's touch was reverent, an act performed for mutual enjoyment.

Martin's lovemaking had been silent, as if noise would break his concentration, impede satisfaction.

Nick's lovemaking was vocal. His breath flung noisily from his lungs. He gasped. He grunted. He whispered words of encouragement—"Oh, God, I like that." He whispered words of praise—"You feel so good."

Martin was controlled, his touch light, his movements rhythmic and predictable.

Nick was spontaneous. His hands gripped and clutched. His body quivered and jerked.

Martin took, coming before she'd been satisfied, leaving her to resort to manual stimulation afterwards.

Nick gave. His mouth moved over hers, stoking her passion. His body pressed against hers—his heartbeat in sync with hers, his breathing merged with hers. His hips where like pistons, driving into her, driving her need higher.

The heat burning inside her became too much to hold. She dug her heels into Nick's ass, and her fingernails into his back, as the passion he'd kindled inside spilled outward.

She screamed.

Nick groaned.

Her body quaked.

Nick's body tensed. His fingers clutched. His cock jerked and spasmed deep inside her.

Time became meaningless, as her total awareness hung on the riotous sensation exploding within her body . . .

As her heart rate returned to normal and Nick's erratic breathing subsided, the final comparison flitted through her mind:

With Martin, Jessie had felt distant.

With Nick, she felt connected.

How in the hell had that happened?

12

As Nick's breathing returned to normal, he realized Jessie was supporting more of his body than he was. He shifted, transferring this weight from her chest to his forearms, resting along-side her shoulders. He brushed his lips against the side of her neck, tasting the slight saltiness dotting her skin.

Saltiness because of his touch, his kiss, his sex.

His cock stirred inside her. He grinned inwardly. Again? Maybe his cock was thinking about more action, but there was no time. He had a flight to catch in a few hours.

Which was too bad because sex had been incredible. Never before had fucking been fun. Sex with Sandy had been serious, intense, making him feel like they were in some sort of competition. Maybe he was competing, considering all the other men that had been in the race without his knowledge.

With Jessie, he was able to take risks, to be imaginative and silly. In short, to be himself. Whatever he felt like being at the moment.

Playful. Naughty. Goofy.

What a novel concept—feeling free to be himself during sex. With a woman who was equally free and fun and silly and naughty.

Very, very, naughty.

He smiled at the thought.

Not wanting to crush Jessie, he pushed his hips away and pulled out of her.

His cock was free.

The connection remained.

Nick glanced at Jessie's face. As if suddenly aware of his gaze, the dreaminess—mixed with something resembling fear—that seemed to flicker in her eyes, was instantly masked. A smile curved her lips and her gaze dropped to the vicinity of his nose.

He recognized the look he'd glimpsed. It was a look that said that the woman under him or on top of him or across from him was feeling more than sex, but trying to hide it.

Or maybe that was just wishful thinking on his part.

It didn't feel like wishful thinking—hell, he didn't even understand why he was wishing for it, given his vow to avoid women. Well, now, he was making a slight correction to the vow.

He was going to avoid the *wrong* type of woman.

And, so far, Jessie felt like the right type.

And speaking of type, he also knew she was the relationship type—he'd known that the night he'd ended up in her bedroom, when she'd cried out for Martin. Just as he'd known that, after being aroused by her naked body in the window, after hearing her throaty plea, after finding himself between her legs, sampling her juices, tasting her need—

His cock lengthened, caressing her thigh and sending a jolt of lust up to his stomach.

That night, he'd desperately wanted to be Martin.

"You okay?" she asked.

Funny question. It was the one *he* usually asked. "Yeah."

"Good."

Her gaze returned to his. All traces of vulnerability had disappeared, replaced by a look completely feline. Her legs slid up and down his ass, her clit brushed up against his cock.

"The doctor seems to still be in the house," she purred.

Nick laughed.

Jessie grinned.

"You want more?" he asked.

"Definitely. And I even have another condom."

Nick chuckled.

He'd barely replaced the used one with the new one before her heels once again dug into his ass, urging him closer.

"All right." He laughed again, appreciating the irony that this was the first time he could remember in a long while that he didn't need it again—though he definitely wanted it—while the woman he was with did.

Maybe he'd have to take a later flight.

Jessie's fingertips circled his cock and wiped all thoughts of travel plans from his mind. And as her fingers guided him back to where she wanted him, and as her hips tilted forward, positioning him at the wet entrance she wanted him to enter, he forgot that he was satisfied.

Lust slammed through him.

His hips met against hers, burying his cock inside her.

She gasped.

He grunted.

And everything became mindless, every action became instinctual.

Her hips, undulating underneath his, set the pace, making him drive into her faster, then slower, then deeper, then more shallow.

Her voice, chanting his name in breathless spurts, pleaded and demanded at the same time, telling him what she needed.

He gripped her ass, holding her still, and she moaned his name; he plundered her mouth, sucked her neck, bit her nipple, and his name slipped from her lips like a shiver; he said her name, urging her onward and upward, and she obliged.

Her body jerked against his.

His name exploded from her mouth, barely decipherable.

Released from her need, Nick was free to go after his own. He pumped furiously.

He held her closer and tighter, needing the heat from her body to merge with his.

He covered her mouth with his, catching her jerky breath, needing the air sustaining her to sustain him.

His body tensed. His cock pulsed.

And all the heat that had been building in his body, erupted inside hers, leaving him shuddering at the loss.

Oddly, that orgasm was better than the first—stronger, more intense, longer-lasting. On a scale of one to ten, definitely a twelve.

"Wow. That was . . . fun," she said.

Using what little air remained in his lungs, Nick laughed.

~~~~

Jessie frowned as Nick's laughter rumbled through her, as his breath bounced off of her shoulder. "What's so funny?"

"Fun? That's it? Please. Don't stroke my ego so."

Jessie smiled. "I'll have you know, that is a major compliment. It was also awesome, spectacular, sinful . . ."

"Okay, okay." Still laughing, Nick pulled out of her, removed the condom, and moved away. "I was just teasing you. That was my word for it as well. One of my words anyway."

She kept her smile in place, struggling between wanting to know what other words he would use to describe what had just happened and wondering if his abrupt departure signaled the end of their rendezvous. She watched him pick up his jeans and walk to the stereo and flick a switch.

Lite jazz filled the room.

Nervousness filled her. She yawned, then stretched.

This was why she never engaged in casual sex. She never knew what the rules were afterwards.

Well, that was only one reason.

The main reason was probably because she felt there were no guarantees that sex would be any good—and what could be more humiliating than having sex for sex's sake and having it be *bad* sex?

Well, she definitely didn't need to worry about bad sex with Nick. Two orgasms in less than an hour. How had that happened?

It used to take Martin an hour to bring her to

orgasm, and sometimes—out of embarrassment for both of them—she faked it. Not that Martin was bad in bed. He was just so . . . serious about sex. It was like, well, another audit he had to perform. He'd never go along with her need for play, for teasing.

Not like Nick.

All he'd had to do is nibble a few bear cookies, play a game or two of doctor, throw in a few smoky glances and hot touches, and a raging inferno had consumed her body.

Who would've thought fun could be such a powerful aphrodisiac?

She sat up, just as Nick, clad only in his half-zipped up jeans, returned and stopped in front of her.

Tissue touched her skin as he wiped the wetness from her thighs and higher. He pulled her dress down, covering the tops of her legs, then slid the straps of her top up her arms and over her shoulders. Reaching behind her, he zipped the back, leaving her fully covered as if he'd never touched her.

Only the comfortable ache and the remaining wetness in her pussy was a pleasant reminder of all that had happened.

Jessie sighed and slid from the table, looking around the room for her sandals. She didn't even remember taking them off. They must be—

Nick took her hand in his and led her to the couch. He sat down and pulled her down onto his lap. "I would invite you into my bed, only I don't have one."

"How can you not have a bed?" she asked. "Seems like that's one of the most important pieces of furniture."

"Yeah, well, my ex-girlfriend thought so, too.

Since everyone but me seemed to be in it, I decided to get a new one."

"Oh . . ." What did one say to that? "I'm sorry."

Nick rubbed her back and placed a light kiss on her forehead. "Don't be. I was over her a long time ago. I just didn't realize how long ago until last week."

Could he mean what she thought he meant? That meeting her had something to do with his realization?

Before she could think of a way to ask him, he changed the subject.

"I wish I could stay the night with you but I have to go."

"This late? Where?"

Too late, she caught herself. She barely knew him. Where he was going was none of her business. Hours of spectacular sex did not give her any right to answers.

Her face felt warm. "Oh, I mean, sure. No problem." She scrambled to get off his lap.

He held her down. "I have to catch a flight to New York—sign the papers on the house I sold."

Jessie relaxed, pleased that he'd told her.

"I'll be back late Sunday night. I'd like to see you."

Happiness welled up in her heart. "I'd like that, too. How about I leave a key out for you?"

"Under the flowerpot?"

"How'd you know?"

Nick laughed. "Because it sounds like you."

She drew back to look at him. "How's that?"

His expression was serious. "Honest, trusting."

"Yeah. I guess so." She lay her head on his chest. "Mmmm. This feels nice . . . Let me know when you have to go."

They sat in silence.

He rubbed her back.

She stroked his arm.

Sitting with Nick felt so . . . nice, so comfortable.

Martin hadn't been big into cuddling, seeing it more as a duty than a delight. Nick seemed content, as if enjoying the feel of her, desiring her touch.

The music played softly in the background.

The silence grew between them.

And still, she felt comfortable.

An advertisement for *The Sin Club* interrupted her peace, forcing her to break the silence. "I was 'sinning' the day I met you."

"Hmmmm?" His voice was relaxed.

"I'd been listening to Dr. Love, taking his advice to be bold, to go for it, to 'sin.' He was right. If I hadn't done it, I wouldn't have met you."

"I'm glad you did . . . I guess I've sinned, too."

"What was your sin?"

"Deciding to take a chance with you."

13

Deciding to take a chance with you.

Nick's words had danced through her mind ever since they'd parted. The promise they held made her glow. She'd barely been able to concentrate, anxiously waiting for his return home.

And now it was Sunday. He'd be here shortly.

Jessie adjusted the pillow behind her back and sipped her wine, letting her gaze circle her bedroom. Her eyes lingered on the window and she smiled. It was hard to believe that one little striptease in this room had changed her life so drastically.

She took another sip of wine and let her gaze move on.

To Teddy, who she would never again think of as an innocent bear.

To her dresser where the red silk scarf sat that she'd used as a blindfold as she'd waited for Martin—

Jessie frowned as she took a gulp of Merlot. Speaking of Martin, he was supposed to have picked up his stuff today and hadn't showed. Not that she was surprised. When was the last time he'd followed through on a commitment he'd made? Heck, he hadn't even opened her please-come-home-and-fuck-me invitation.

"He didn't think it was 'important,'" she muttered, bracketing the word "important" in the air with her fingers.

She giggled. "Yeah, well, Nick thought it was important. I gave him an invitation he couldn't resist." She giggled again, this time until tears sprang to her eyes. As the laughter ended, she reached for the bottle on her nightstand, and paused.

Maybe she shouldn't have any more to drink. Oh, one more glass. There was plenty left for Nick.

Or maybe not.

As she tilted the bottle over her glass, nothing came out. Damn. She set both the glass and the bottle on the nightstand. How had that happened? How had she managed to finish off the whole bottle?

Guess she was tipsier than she'd thought. Well, thank God Nick's plane was late. It'd give her some time to sober up and be alert and ready when he came in.

Nick.

Just the mention of his name made her body hot. The things they'd done—she'd never thought a child's game could be so erotic.

The things they were going to do . . .

Jessie slid under the covers and closed her eyes, letting her mind replay the surprise she'd planned for Nick. Another striptease.

Only, this time, instead of him standing outside her window, he'd be inside . . .

Nick sits on her bed. Wearing a smile and the same slinky

red gown he'd first seen her in, Jessie strolls and struts in front of him, gyrating her hips and . . .

She burrowed deeper under the covers.

. . . running her hands down her body. She shimmies up to him and, holding a breast in each hand, she bends to within centimeters of his mouth and lets her nipples graze his lips. Then, she stands and twirls around, giving him a view of her ass, before sitting on his lap . . .

Jessie yawned. Her body felt so tired . . .

. . . His cock is as hard as a rock behind the zipper of his pants. And, as she rubs her ass against him—up and down, side to side—he grows even harder. He wants to touch her, but he can't. He asks . . .

. . . asks . . .

. . . asks . . .

"Is it okay if I stay?" he whispered in her ear.

Jessie stirred, feeling an arm across her waist and a cock pressed against her ass. Nick's *hard* cock. She smiled and her eyes fluttered open, taking in the pitch black room, then drifted shut again.

She must've fallen asleep.

"You came," she said.

"Shhhh. Go back to sleep. We'll talk in the morning."

She didn't want to go back to sleep. She tried to open her eyes again. But she was sleepy. "Okay," she said, scooting back against Nick.

He gasped.

She smiled . . .

. . . asks, "Is it okay if I stay?"

She places her hands on his thighs for better leverage and rubs her ass against his cock harder, faster. "You're not going anywhere," she says.

His breath is ragged in her ear.

His chest is tense against her back. "Do you want me, Nick?"

"Oh, God, yes."

She likes the pain of need she hears in his voice. It excites her, makes her feel feminine and powerful and desirable. But she's had enough of the games.

She wants him, too.

She rises and turns to face him, pulling him to his feet. Unbuttoning and unzipping his jeans, she pulls his jeans and underwear over his hips. Her body throbs at the sight of him.

As usual, he is ready for her.

She pushes him onto the bed and climbs on top of him and . . .

The bed dipped sharply to the right seconds before a loud crash yanked Jessie out of the dream. She shot straight up and turned around, facing the bedroom door.

Her mouth dropped open.

The hallway light illuminated Nick, standing in front of the closet door, completely naked, broken glass from the lamp on the floor in front of him.

Martin stood, wearing only a tank undershirt and black socks.

Jessie closed her eyes.

When she reopened her eyes, both men still stood naked in front of her.

What the hell was going on here?

"He kissed my neck," Martin yelled, scrubbing the back of his neck with his hand. "Jessie, give me the baseball bat."

"I'd love to give you the bat, Martin," she said, unmoving. "What are you—"

Totally missing her sarcasm, he held out his hand impatiently. "Well?"

Nick reached down to pick up his jeans.

"Nick, don't—"

"Don't move," said Martin to Nick. He ducked under the bed and picked up the bat. "Jessie, call the police."

Nick put on his jeans and bent to pick up his shirt.

Martin stood and waved the bat. "I said don't move."

Nick looked at him in disgust and continued dressing. "What is it with you two and bats?"

Fully dressed, Nick dismissed Martin and turned an accusing glare to Jessie. "Now I understand why you said fucking me was 'fun.'"

"Wait a minute, you know him, Jessie? You *had sex* with him? How could—"

"What are you talking about, Nick?"

Nick's lips twisted. "It was all a big game to you."

"Nick, I don't know what's going on here. I was waiting for you and—"

"Really? And were you waiting for Martin, too?"

Jessie's confusion gave way to anger. How dare he accuse her of fucking both of them.

"My God, he knows my name! Jessie, how—"

"Martin, shut up. I can only deal with one idiot at a time." Jessie jumped out of bed and grabbed her robe.

"Answer the question, Jessie," said Nick.

She whirled toward Nick, her blood boiling. "I wasn't waiting for Martin. He was supposed to come over earlier."

She glared at Martin.

"Well. Thanks for answering the question. It's been . . .'fun.'"

"Oh, for crying out loud," Jessie said, placing a

hand on her forehead.

Nick turned and stalked out of the room. She heard him stomp down the stairs.

Seconds later, the front door slammed.

"Damn it," said Jessie, running a hand through her hair. She took a deep breath and turned to Martin. "What the hell are you doing here?"

"I came to get my stuff."

"Your 'stuff' is not in my bed."

"You invited me into your bed."

"I did not!"

"I asked if I could stay and you pressed your bottom against me then whispered, 'you came.'"

Oh. Right. But she'd thought he was Nick.

"Obviously, you were expecting someone else. I *thought* we should give us another chance, but . . ." He shook his head. "I don't think it's going to work, Jessie."

"I'm glad we finally agree, Martin."

He motioned towards the stairs with the bat. "Who was that, Jessie?"

"Oh, geez, enough, Martin."

She stalked forward, picked up his pants, shirt, and tie and thrust them into his free hand. She yanked the bat out of his other hand. "That is my new neighbor, whom I met the night that you failed to open the letter I sent to you by courier."

She ushered him out of the bedroom and down the stairs as she talked.

"Jessie, that's awfully fast. You're probably rebounding. I don't think—"

"Martin, I don't care what you think. We. Are. Over." They were at the front door. "I want my key and I will send you your stuff."

She waited for Martin to dress, then held out her hand for her key.

He sighed, dug into his pocket and took it off his key chain. He handed it to her. "Jessie—"

"Thank you and good-bye, Martin." She opened the front door, pushed him out, and shut the door behind him.

As she listened to him clatter down the front stairs, she leaned against the door. No sooner had she closed her eyes, than there was a knock on her door.

"For God's sake, Martin!" She yanked the door open. "Leave me—"

It wasn't Martin.

Her heart jangled in her chest. She forced herself to frown. "What are you doing here, Nick?"

"I came to let you explain."

"Don't do me any favors."

"I'd like to hear it."

"Well, I don't want to explain it."

Nick glared.

Jessie glared.

"What was Martin doing here?"

"He came to get his stuff."

"His stuff was in your bed?"

Their thought processes were in sync. If she'd been in a better frame of mind, she would've appreciated the irony. But fury didn't set the mood for humor. "He was supposed to come earlier. I'd assumed he'd forgotten. I was waiting for you, trying to stay up, but I drank a bottle of wine and got sleepy."

She crossed her arms. "Next thing I know, my room has been invaded by The Two Stooges."

Nick's lips twitched.

Jessie's lips tightened. "How could you have thought I'd sleep with Martin?"

He raised a brow. "Maybe when I caught him in bed with you?"

He had a point. "Well, why would I be stupid enough to invite Martin over the same night you were supposed to come by?"

"The question did occur to me."

She sighed in frustration. "Why didn't you let me explain?"

"I am now."

Oh. Right, again.

"Look, I overreacted. But, come on, Jessie. If the roles were reversed, wouldn't you have reacted the same?"

He had another point. God, she was beginning to hate being wrong. "No."

"No?"

"I would've yanked the covers back and ordered both of you out, then picked up your clothes and thrown them out the window, while calling both of you every name in the book, and telling you never to come back, then I would've called the police and obtained a restraining order . . ."

Jessie paused for breath.

Nick's mouth hung open.

Jessie smiled sweetly. "Sorry. Go on."

"Uh . . ."

She waited.

"Like I said, I wasn't thinking, rationally—that is. My mind instantly latched onto the belief that you'd just been having fun with me—in a bad away—that you'd been toying with me."

"Nick, I'm not . . . her."

"I know," he said softly. "That's why I like you."

Jessie remained silent, ignoring the flush of pleasure caused by his words, refusing to give into the pull of sweet-talk.

Nick grinned. "You have to admit, it was kind of funny."

Jessie's lips quirked. "Yeah . . . it was, I guess." Enough had been said. All was forgiven. "You want to come inside?"

"Yeah, under one condition." Jessie frowned. "What condition?"

"That you promise to shave your hairy chest."

"Hairy—" Oh. Right. Martin's chest. He must've slipped his arms around Martin when he'd slid into bed.

Her laughter prevented her from finishing the sentence. "

"Well? Will—"

Her kiss prevented *him* from finishing his sentence.

ABOUT THE AUTHOR

Rachelle Chase is an award-winning romance author, business consultant, speaker, and model who's appeared on national television—CBS, as well as "The Morning Show with Mike and Juliet"—plus national radio shows, including "Playboy Radio," the "Hip-Hop Connection," and the "Jordan Rich Show."

An excerpt from "Out of Control," a novella in SECRETS VOLUME 13, was used in ON WRITING ROMANCE, published by Writer's Digest Books, to illustrate how to effectively heighten sexual tension in a romance book.

Published works include:

KICKING THE BUCKET LIST (memoir)—
available 2015
A SINFUL FIANCÉ (The Sin Club Book 4)—
available Spring 2015
HOT DREAMS—available Summer 2015
"The Firefighter Wears Prada" in MEN ON FIRE
SEX LOUNGE
A SINFUL STRIPTEASE (The Sin Club Book 1)
A SINFUL PHONE CALL (The Sin Club Book 2)
A SINFUL PROPOSITION (The Sin Club Book 3)
"Out of Control" in SECRETS VOLUME 13

Read more or sign up for her newsletter at
www.RachelleChase.com.

Here's a hot sneak peek at Rachelle Chase's

A Sinful Phone Call (The Sin Club Book 2),

available now . . .

1

"Hi, Shawn. I'm the woman who was wearing the short red dress, standing on the corner."

Damn.

Cringing at the words she'd just blurted, Sharice jabbed the pound key on the cell phone keypad to delete the voicemail message she'd just recorded. As the digital voice walked her through the instructions to rerecord her message, she stared out the windshield of her Lexus, idly noticing the after-eleven crowd in line in front of the new nightclub, Tantrum. Defying the chilly October air, the women wore their spaghetti-strap tops and tightest skirts, while standing proud in their three-inch strappy sandals.

She tried again.

"Hi, Shawn . . . This is Sharice. I met you outside of Tantrum last Friday. I was talking to my friend when you shouted your number out the window . . ."

My God. Are the pickings for a night of sex so slim that I have to resort to this? Just hang up.

"... and ..."

Hang up.

"... well ..."

Hang the fuck up.

But, damn, that man had been on her mind all week. It was once again Friday evening, and she somehow found herself cruising down the street in front of the club where they'd met. Her favorite song played on the radio—Kid Ink, crooning about how he was going to push her panties to the side—and got her all hot and bothered.

The same song had been playing softly from the depths of Shawn's Lex that night, too. Surely, that must be a sign. Just as the fact that his gleaming red car, identical to hers, was a sign. A sign that, unlike her last boyfriend, Darrell, and his 1990 Honda Civic, Shawn might actually treat her to dinner, instead of always crying broke. And Shawn's voice, as he'd practically begged her to call him, had sounded like liquid sex. That had been another sign.

The voice was a definite positive for a night of hot sex. For, if his technique was sad, she could just ask him to talk—and that sweet, slow, sexy tone would make up for any lack of finesse.

Sharice paused, about to delete her message again, when the song faded out on the radio and Tommy "Dr. Love" Jones came on.

"Now, that's a sinful song, isn't it?" He laughed. "It's definitely telling you to go out and sin, though not necessarily the way I'm advocating. I'm urging you, KPSX listeners, to go out and go for what you want, sin. Your happiness is just a sin away ..."

Dr. Love was right. It was about time she "sinned." That is, do something she'd never done before. She turned her attention back to the phone.

". . . Call me at 510-555-1201," she finished.

Sharice clicked her phone off and tossed it onto the passenger seat, surprised to feel herself shaking from surplus adrenaline. How ridiculous that something as simple as calling a guy would spark the fight-or-flight response. On the other hand, maybe it wasn't so ridiculous, since she *never* called men first, period. She always waited for them to call her. Hell, she was no fool—she lived by the book *He's Just Not That Into You,* which was co-authored by Greg Behrendt.

Hence, she was committing a double sin—she was calling a guy first and she was calling a guy she hadn't even really met. And the only reason she'd broken her rule this time was because, well, it was kind of hard for a guy who didn't have her name or number to call her back.

So now what?

The line outside the club had grown another twelve feet since she'd arrived. Sharice did not do lines. Craning her neck forward, she looked to see if John was at the door. Yep. There he was, his bald, peanut-shaped head glistening in the soft light. He'd let her slide to the front of the line. There'd be no waiting tonight.

Sharice sighed. So what if she got in the club? Somewhere in between the time that she'd pulled out of her garage and pulled into this parking spot, Tantrum had lost its appeal. The effort it would take to make meaningless small talk with a dozen or more men, in hopes of meeting one she wanted to take home for the night seemed like too much effort. Kind of like finding her contact lens in the Pacific Ocean.

She'd been feeling like that a lot lately, which was why she'd been celibate for months. *Six* months, to be exact.

A group of loud-talking sistahs—whose long hair did a better job of covering their asses than their skirts did—sauntered past the car. Did they really think they looked good?

Stop being so bitchy.

She should just go home. Her attitude was not male-magnet material.

But she didn't want to go home. Friday night was a prime party night, for crying out loud. And it was time for her to get her game back on track.

Sharice pressed the pad of her finger against the screen, turning up the radio. The deep voice of Dr. Love filled the car.

". . . Good luck, man . . . You're on, Jessie. What's your sin?"

Jessie giggled.

Sharice rolled her eyes.

"Well, a couple of months ago, I did a striptease for my boyfriend. It was something I'd always wanted to do, but had never done before . . ."

Dr. Love made a sound of approval.

Sharice snorted. "That ain't nothing. I've done a hundred stripteases."

". . . only it wasn't my boyfriend who saw it. It was my neighbor."

"Damn. I haven't done *that,*" said Sharice.

Dr. Love laughed.

Jessie laughed. ". . . needless to say, the boyfriend's out and my neighbor is in."

"He's 'in'? Literally or figuratively?" asked Dr. Love.

Jessie and Dr. Love shared a chuckle.

Sharice joined in.

"Let's just say he's the new man in my life. Our relationship is wonderful. He—"

Sharice snorted. "I was feeling you until you ruined things with a 'relationship.'" She pressed the screen again, cutting Jessie off in mid-sentence; Sharice shook her head. A person had a better chance of winning the lottery than ending up in a relationship that worked. What was up with most women who were desperate for the big R? Sharice had tried that, twice, believing that she'd found *the one* each time. Instead, she'd discovered Malcolm had been living on the down low, sleeping with men behind her back. And Darrell had been sleeping with anything in a skirt, including whichever of her so-called friends he could get into bed—Sharice's bed.

Nope. She was through with that. Fool me once, shame on you; fool me twice, shame on me. Well, she was not going to be anyone's fool anymore. So now she just looked for a brotha for a good time.

But, for some reason, the "good times" were feeling fewer and farther in between. And Sharice's attitude was getting more and more frustrated. Not to mention her libido. She shrugged, throwing off her depressing thoughts.

Well, she might as well go inside the club. As she reached for her keys, her cell phone rang.

She glanced at the display on her cell. It was Shawn. Sharice grinned, no longer nervous now that she was back on familiar ground—being pursued.

www.ingramcontent.com/pod-product-compliance
Lightning Source LLC
Chambersburg PA
CBHW020627130626
46552CB00003B/1109